Hans Christian Andersen Fairy Tales

Selected & Illustrated by
Lisbeth Zwerger

Translated by Anthea Bell

Picture Book Studio

A Michael Neugebauer Book.

Copyright © 1991, Neugebauer Press, Salzburg.

Published in the United States by Picture Book Studio, Saxonville, Massachusetts.

Distributed in the United States by Simon & Schuster.

Distributed in Canada by Vanwell Publishing, St.Catharines, Ontario.

Printed in Hong Kong.

Library of Congress Cataloging in Publication Data

Andersen, H.C. (Hans Christian), 1805–1875.

[Tales. English. Selections]

Hans Christian Andersen Fairy Tales

selected and illustrated by Lisbeth Zwerger; translated by Anthea Bell.

p. cm.

Translation of: Hans Christian Andersen Märchen,

ausgewählt und illustriert von Lisbeth Zwerger.

Summary: eight tales chosen by the illustrator,

winner of the 1990 Hans Christian Andersen Medal for lifetime achievement

in the field of illustration for children.

ISBN 0-88708-182-7

1. Fairy tales—Denmark. 2. Children's stories, Danish-Translations into English.

3. Children's stories, English-Translations from Danish.

[1. Fairy tales. 2. Short stories.]

I. Zwerger, Lisbeth, ill. II. Title.

PZ8.A54 1991

[E]—dc20 91-13132

CIP

AC

The Sandman 7

The Emperor's New Clothes 29

The Princess & the Pea 35

The Tinderbox 39

The Rose Tree Regiment 49

The Naughty Boy 53

The Jumpers 57

The Little Match Girl 61

The Sandman

No one in the world knows as many stories as the Sandman. Yes indeed, he tells really wonderful stories!

The Sandman comes in the evening, when children are sitting at the table, or perhaps on their stools. He comes upstairs very quietly in his stocking feet, opens the door softly, and then he sprinkles the finest of sand into their eyes. They don't see him, because they can hardly keep their eyes open. He creeps quietly up behind them, blows gently on their necks, and they begin to feel sleepy. The Sandman does them no harm, for he is kind to children. He just wants them to be quiet, and they are more likely to be quiet once they have been put to bed. He wants them to be quiet so that he can tell them stories.

Once the children are asleep the Sandman sits on their beds. He wears lovely clothes and a silk coat, but what color it is I cannot say, for it looks green, red, or blue depending which way he turns. He has an umbrella under each arm. One has pictures on it, and he holds it over good children to make them dream of wonderful things all night long. The other has no pictures on it at all. He holds that one over naughty children, and then they sleep heavily and have had no dreams at all when they wake in the morning.

Well, now let's hear the stories the Sandman once told a little boy called Hjalmar. He came to see Hjalmar every day for a week, and told him some very fine stories, seven of them altogether, because there are seven days in a week.

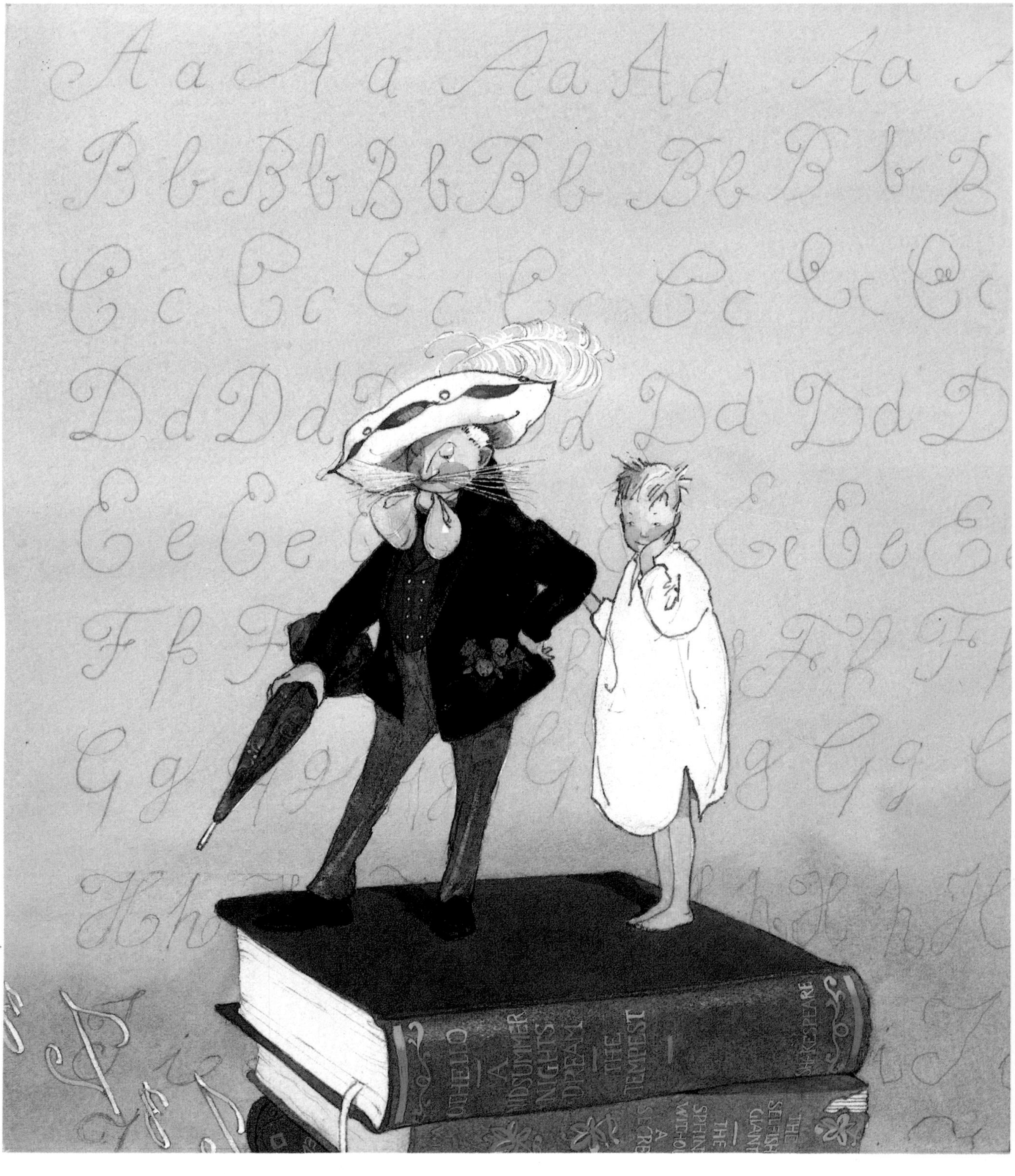
A MIDSUMMER NIGHTS DREAM
THE TEMPEST
SHAKESPEARE

"Now then," said the Sandman one evening, when he had put Hjalmar to bed, "I'm going to make your room look pretty." And all the flowers in their pots grew and became tall trees with long branches that went all along the ceiling and down the walls, so that the whole room looked like a beautiful bower. The branches were covered with flowers, and every one of them was even lovelier than a rose. They were wonderfully fragrant too, and if you ate one it tasted sweeter than jam. Golden fruit gleamed among the branches, and buns full of raisins hung on them too. It was a wonderful sight. But then a pitiful wailing was heard coming from the drawer of the table where Hjalmar had put his school books.

"What's all this?" asked the Sandman, and he went to the table and opened the drawer. It was Hjalmar's slate making the noise! One of the figures in the sum on it was wrong, and all the others were pushing and shoving until the whole slate was in danger of falling to bits. The slate pencil was leaping and jumping about like a little dog on the end of its string, trying to help correct the sum, but it couldn't. More wailing came from Hjalmar's exercise book—it was a really miserable sound. Each page had a capital letter and a small letter written on it, as examples to be copied out in rows. Other letters stood next to these handsome ones and thought they looked the same, but they were the letters Hjalmar had written, and they were lying about all over the place, as if they had fallen over the penciled line instead of standing on it properly.

"Look, this is the way to stand!" said the handsome copybook letters. "You want to slope this way, with a nice flourish to you!"

"We only wish we could," said the letters Hjalmar had written, "but we feel so poorly! We can't!"

"Then you'd better have some medicine to make you better," said the Sandman.

"No, no!" cried the letters, standing up straight at once.

"Well, I can see we won't get any stories told this evening," said the Sandman. "I'd better drill these letters. One, two! One, two!" he shouted, drilling the letters until they stood up as straight and handsome as copybook letters can.

However, when Hjalmar looked at them in the morning after the Sandman had left, they were just as bad as ever.

TUESDAY

As soon as Hjalmar was in bed the Sandman touched all the furniture in the room with his little magic wand, and at once it began to talk. All the pieces of furniture were talking about themselves, except for the spittoon, which kept silent. He wished they wouldn't be so vain, chattering on and on about themselves with never a thought for him. He just stood humbly in the corner letting people spit in him.

There was a big picture in a gilded frame hanging over the chest of drawers. It was a landscape, a picture showing tall old trees, flowers in the grass, and a great river winding its way through the forest, passing many castles on its way to the open sea.

The Sandman turned his magic wand on the painting, and the birds in the picture began to sing, the branches of the trees swayed, and the clouds moved across the sky. You could see their shadows passing over the landscape.

Then the Sandman lifted little Hjalmar up to the frame, and he climbed right into the picture and stood there in the tall grass. The sun was shining down on him through the branches of the trees. He ran to the river and climbed into a little boat moored there. It was painted red and white, with sails shining like silver. Six swans, all with golden crowns around their necks and bright blue stars on their heads, drew the boat past the green woods where trees told tales of robbers and witches, and the flowers talked about the pretty little elves and the stories they had heard from butterflies.

Beautiful fish with scales like gold and silver swam after the boat. Every now and then they jumped, and there was a splash in the water. Long lines of red and blue birds, both large and small, flew after them. Midges danced in the air, and the cockchafer boomed. They all wanted to follow Hjalmar, and they all had stories to tell.

What a boating trip that was! Sometimes the woods were thick and dark, sometimes they were like a lovely garden full of sunshine and flowers, with great castles of glass and marble among them. Princesses stood on the castle balconies, and they were all little girls Hjalmar knew well and used to play with. They stretched out their hands, holding the nicest sugar pigs you could buy, and Hjalmar took one end of each sugar pig as he sailed past while the princess held tight to the other, so that each had a bit of it. The princess had the smaller half of the sugar pig and Hjalmar had the larger half! Little princes stood on guard outside every castle, shouldering their golden swords and throwing raisins and tin soldiers. They were real princes and no mistake!

Hjalmar sailed on, and the boat seemed to pass sometimes through woods, sometimes through great halls or a town. He sailed through the town where the nurse who used to look after him when he was a baby lived. She loved him very much. She nodded and waved, and sang a little song she had made up herself and sent him:

> I often think of you, dear child,
> My darling little boy!
> To kiss your mouth, your brow so mild,
> Your cheeks, was all my joy.
> I heard your first words, shared your mirth,
> But then we had to part.
> May God protect you here on earth,
> The angel of my heart.

The birds all sang too, and the flowers danced on their stalks, and the old trees nodded as if the Sandman were telling them stories as well.

WEDNESDAY

The rain was pouring down outside in torrents. Hjalmar could hear it even in his sleep, and when the Sandman opened the window there was water up to the sill. The floods were like a lake outside, and a splendid ship was moored close to the house.

"Would you like to come sailing, little Hjalmar?" asked the Sandman. "You can travel to foreign lands tonight and be back again in the morning."

All at once Hjalmar was on the wonderful ship, dressed in his Sunday best, and immediately the weather cleared. They sailed down the streets, cruised around the church, and soon they were out on the high seas. They sailed so far that they couldn't see the shore any more, and then they saw a flock of storks flying from land on their way to the warm countries. The storks flew in single file, and they had all come a very long way. One of them was so tired that his wings could hardly carry him any more. He was the last in line, and soon he was lagging far behind the others. At last he sank lower and lower, with outstretched wings. He beat his wings once or twice more, but it was no good. His feet touched the ship's rigging, he fell down past the sail, and he landed on the deck.

The cabin boy picked him up and put him in the henhouse, with the hens and ducks and turkeys. The poor stork stood among them feeling very downcast.

"Look at that funny bird!" said the hens.

And the turkey puffed himself up as big as he could and asked the stork his name, while the ducks waddled about, nudging each other and going, "Quack! Quack!"

The stork told them about the hot lands of Africa, and the Pyramids, and the ostrich who runs about the desert like a wild horse, but the ducks couldn't understand a word he said. They just nudged each other again, quacking, "Isn't he silly? Isn't he silly?"

"He certainly is!" gobbled the turkey. The stork said nothing, but he thought about Africa.

"You have an elegant pair of long legs there!" said the turkey. "What did they cost you—a yard?"

"Quack, quack, quack!" went the ducks, giggling, but the stork looked as if he hadn't heard.

"Well, you might have joined in the laughter!" said the turkey. "I mean, it was very funny! Or perhaps it was beneath your notice? Can't take a joke, I see! Well, let's go on amusing ourselves!" And the hens clucked and the ducks quacked, thinking themselves extremely witty.

But Hjalmar went over to the henhouse, opened the door and called the stork, who hopped out on deck. He was feeling rested now, and nodded to Hjalmar as if to thank him. Then he spread his wings and flew away to the hot countries, while the hens clucked, the ducks quacked, and the turkey went bright red in the face.

"Watch out, or we'll make you into soup tomorrow!" said Hjalmar, and next moment he woke up in his own little bed. What a wonderful voyage the Sandman had sent him on that night!

THURSDAY

"Now," said the Sandman, "don't be afraid, and I'll show you a little mouse!" He held out his hand, with the pretty little creature in it. "She's come to invite you to a wedding," he said. "Two mice are getting married tonight. They live under your mother's dining room floor, and I believe they have a very nice mousehole there."

"But how can I get into a little mousehole under the floor?" asked Hjalmar.

"Leave that to me!" said the Sandman. "I'll shrink you!" And he touched Hjalmar with his magic wand. Hjalmar immediately shrank, becoming smaller and smaller until he was no bigger than a finger. "You can borrow the tin soldier's clothes. I think they'll fit you, and a uniform looks fine at a party!"

"Oh yes!" said Hjalmar, and in a moment he was dressed like a smart tin soldier.

"Will you be so good as to sit in your mother's thimble?" said the little mouse. "Then I can have the pleasure of pulling you along!"

"How kind of you to go to so much trouble, ma'am!" said Hjalmar, and they drove off to the mouse wedding.

First of all they went down a long passage under the floor, only just big enough for the thimble to get through it. The whole passage was lighted by burning torches made of bits of rotten wood.

"Doesn't it smell nice down here?" said the mouse who was pulling Hjalmar along in the thimble. "The whole passage has been carpeted with bacon rind. What could be better?"

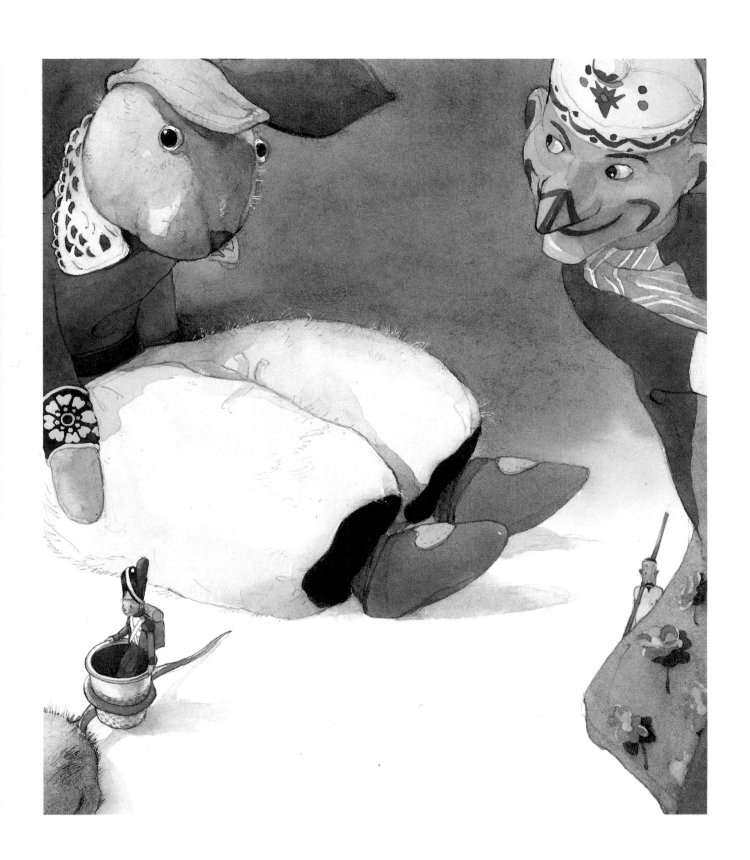

Then they came into the room where the wedding was to be held. All the little lady mice stood on the right, whispering as if they were making fun of each other. All the gentlemen mice stood on the left, stroking their whiskers with their paws. And the happy couple was in the middle of the room, standing on a scooped-out cheese rind and kissing each other lovingly in front of the whole company, because they were already engaged and now they were about to be married.

More guests kept arriving. The mice were in danger of trampling one another, and the bridal couple had placed themselves in the doorway so that you could get neither in nor out. The whole room had been carpeted with bacon rind, like the passage, and that was all there was to eat, except for a pea which was the wedding cake. A little mouse who was a member of the family had nibbled the happy couple's names in it, or rather their initials, so that made it very special.

All the mice said it was a wonderful wedding, and they had found the conversation most entertaining.

Then Hjalmar rode home. He felt he had certainly been to a very grand party, even if it meant shrinking to a size where he could wear the tin soldier's uniform.

"You wouldn't believe how many grown-up people would like to get their hands on me," said the Sandman. "Especially people who have done something bad. 'Dear Sandman,' they say, 'we can't get a wink of sleep, we lie awake all night seeing our evil deeds sitting on the bed like ugly little gnomes, sprinkling hot water over us. Please come and drive them away so that we can get some sleep!' Then they sigh deeply, and say, 'We'll be happy to pay you. Good night, Sandman! You'll find the money on the window sill.' But I don't offer such things for money," said the Sandman.

"What are we going to do tonight?" asked Hjalmar.

"Well, I wonder if you'd like to go to another wedding? It won't be the same as last night's. Your sister's big boy doll Herman is going to marry the other doll, Bertha. It's the doll's birthday, too, so there will be lots of presents."

"I know!" said Hjalmar. "Whenever the dolls need new clothes my sister gives either a birthday party or a wedding for them. They must have had about a hundred weddings!"

"Yes, but tonight is the hundred-and-first, and after a hundred-and-one they can't get married any more, so tonight's will be a very fine wedding indeed," said the Sandman. "Look over there!"

Hjalmar looked at the table and saw that there were lights in the windows of the little cardboard doll's house, while all the tin soldiers were presenting arms outside it. The bride and groom were sitting on the floor, leaning on the table leg and looking very thoughtful—no doubt for good reasons. But the Sandman, wearing Grandmother's black blouse as a gown, married them. When the marriage ceremony was over, all the furniture in the room struck up the following beautiful song. It had been written by the pencil, and had a tune that was like the rat-a-tat-tat of drums.

> *Our song like the blowing wind will roam*
> *And find the bride and groom at home.*
> *Their heads held high, their thoughts refined,*
> *All made of leather—the very best kind.*
> *Though blows the wind, though stormy weather,*
> *Three cheers for the couple—now all together!*

Then it was time for the wedding presents. The dolls had asked their friends not to give them anything to eat, because they were in love, and they could live on love.

"Shall we go into the country or travel abroad for our honeymoon?" asked the bridegroom. They turned for advice to the swallow, who had traveled widely, and the old hen who had hatched out five broods of chicks. The swallow told them about the beautiful warm lands where bunches of grapes hang huge and heavy, where the air is mild and the mountains are tinged with colors never seen here.

"But they don't have cabbages there!" said the hen. "I spent a summer in the country with my chicks, and there was a gravel pit where we could go and scratch about. We could get into a garden where cabbages grew too. They were lovely green cabbages! I can't imagine anything nicer."

"One cabbage stalk looks exactly like the next, if you ask me," said the swallow, "and the weather here is often so bad!"

"You get used to it," said the hen.

"But it's cold here. There are frosts!"

"They're good for the cabbages," said the hen. "Anyway, we sometimes get warm weather too. Didn't we have a summer four years ago that went on for five whole weeks, and it was so hot you could hardly breathe? And we don't get all those nasty poisonous creatures you find abroad. There are no robbers here either. Anyone who doesn't think our country the finest in the world is a rotten scoundrel and doesn't deserve to be here at all," said the hen, bursting into tears. "I've traveled too, you know! I've been all of twelve miles in a coop! Traveling is no fun at all, I can assure you!"

"That hen is talking sense!" said the doll Bertha. "I'd rather not go mountaineering either. Up one side and down another! No, let's go to the gravel pit and walk in the garden where the cabbages grow."

And that was what they did.

SATURDAY

"Are you going to tell me a story?" asked little Hjalmar as soon as the Sandman had put him to bed.

"We won't have time for stories this evening," said the Sandman, holding his pretty umbrella over him. "Look at these Chinese people!" And indeed, the whole umbrella looked like a Chinese bowl, with blue trees, and pointed bridges with little Chinese people standing on them and nodding their heads. "We must have the whole world spick and span for tomorrow," said the Sandman, "because tomorrow is Sunday, and that's a holy day. I must go over to the church tower to see if the little brownies who live there are shining up the bells to make them ring well. I must go out to the fields to see if the wind is blowing the dust off the grass and leaves. And most important of all, I must take all the stars down and polish them! I'll collect them in my apron, but they must be numbered first, and so must their holes in the sky, so that they can go back into their proper places, or they won't stay put and we shall have too many shooting stars falling one after another!"

"Now you listen to me, Mr. Sandman," said an old portrait which hung on the wall near Hjalmar's bed. "I'm Hjalmar's great-grandfather, and I'd like to thank you for telling the lad stories, but you mustn't confuse him! Stars cannot be taken down and polished! Stars are heavenly bodies like the earth, and that's the beauty of them!"

"Thank you, old great-grandfather," said the Sandman. "Thank you very much. You are the head of the family, and a very old head indeed! But I'm even older, you know. I'm an old heathen, and I was known to the Greeks and Romans as the god of dreams. I've been in the grandest of houses, and I go there still. I know how to deal with both great and small. Very well, you can have your say now!"

"I see a person isn't even allowed to speak his mind these days!" said the old portrait.

And with that Hjalmar woke up.

"Good evening," said the Sandman, and Hjalmar nodded, jumping up to turn his great-grandfather's portrait to the wall so that it wouldn't interrupt the way it had interrupted yesterday.

"Now, tell me some stories!" he said. "Tell me the story about the five green peas who lived in one pod, and the one about the frog who would a-wooing go, and the one about the darning needle who thought herself so fine that she imagined she was a sewing needle!"

"You can have too much of a good thing," said the Sandman. "I want to show you something else tonight. I'm going to show you my brother. He is a Sandman too, but he never visits anyone more than once, and then he takes that person up on his horse and tells him stories. He knows only two stories, one more wonderful than anyone in the world can imagine, and one so terrible that—well, there's no describing it!" And the Sandman lifted little Hjalmar up to the window and said, "Look, there's my brother, the other Sandman. He is also called Death. You see, he isn't as frightening as they paint him in picture books, where he's nothing but bones. No, he has silver braid on his coat and wears a very fine military uniform, with a black velvet cape flying out behind him and his horse. See how he gallops along!"

And Hjalmar watched the other Sandman ride by, taking people both young and old up on his horse. He put some of them in front of him and some of them behind him, but first he asked what their reports were like.

They all said they had good reports.

"Well, let me see for myself," said he, and so they had to show him their reports. All the people with "Very Good" or "Outstanding" on their reports were placed in front of Death on the horse, and heard the beautiful story, but those who had reports saying "Moderate" or "Poor" were placed behind Death and had to listen to the terrible story. They trembled and wept and tried to jump off the horse, but they couldn't: it was as if they were stuck fast to it.

"I think Death is the best Sandman of all," said Hjalmar. "I'm not afraid of him."

"And I hope you never will be!" said the Sandman. "Just make sure you get a good report!"

"Very educational!" muttered great-grandfather's portrait. "Well, a person should be allowed to speak his mind. It comes in useful." And he was satisfied.

Those are the stories the Sandman told Hjalmar, and perhaps he will tell you some more himself tonight.

The Emperor's New Clothes

*M*any years ago there was an Emperor who thought fine new clothes were so important that he spent all his money on them. He did not care about his army, or going to the theatre, or hunting in the forest, except as opportunities to show off his new clothes. He had a different suit for every time of day, and while people will often say of a king, "He is in the council chamber," they said of this Emperor, "He is in his dressing room."

The great city where he lived was a prosperous place, and many visitors came daily to see it. One day, however, two rascally swindlers arrived in town, pretending to be weavers and claiming to make the most beautiful cloth you can imagine. Not only were the colors and patterns of the cloth amazingly lovely, they said, but clothes made of it had the wonderful property of remaining invisible to anyone who was either unfit for his job or remarkably stupid.

"Those must be marvelous clothes indeed," thought the Emperor. "If I wore them I could find out which people in my lands are unfit for the positions they hold. I could tell who was clever and who was stupid! I must have that cloth made for me at once!" And he gave the two swindlers a great deal of money to begin work.

So they set up two looms, and pretended to be working, but in fact they were not weaving at all. They said they needed the finest silk and the most precious gold thread, all of which they pocketed themselves, and they worked at their empty looms until late into the night.

"I wonder how my cloth is coming along?" thought the Emperor. He felt slightly alarmed when he remembered that a stupid man, or one unfit for his position, wouldn't be able to see it; he didn't think he need fear for himself, but all the same he decided to send someone else to see how the work was going. All the people in town knew about the wonderful powers of the cloth, and they were all eager to find out how clever or how stupid their neighbors were.

"I'll send my honest old Minister to call on the weavers," thought the Emperor. "He's the best person to see what the cloth looks like, for he is very clever, and no one could be better fitted for his post!"

Well, the good old Minister went into the hall where the two swindlers were sitting working at their empty looms. "Lord preserve us!" thought the old Minister, opening his eyes very wide, "I can't see anything at all!" But he didn't say so.

The two swindlers asked him to be so good as to come closer. Wasn't the pattern very fine, they asked, and weren't the colors beautiful? As they spoke they pointed to the empty loom, and the poor old Minister kept staring, but he could see nothing at all, since there was nothing there. "Dear me!" he thought. "Can it be that I'm stupid? I never thought so myself. Well, no one must know of this! Am I unfit for my post? It will never do for me to confess that I can't see the cloth!"

"Haven't you anything to say?" asked one of the swindlers, pretending to go on weaving.

"Oh yes, it's very nice! Really splendid!" said the old Minister, peering through his glasses. "That pattern! Those colors! Yes, I'll tell the Emperor I like it very much indeed!"

"Delighted to hear it!" said the two weavers, and then they told him what the colors were and described the unusual pattern. The old Minister listened carefully so that he could tell the Emperor all about it, and so he did.

Then the two swindlers asked for more money, and more silk and gold thread, saying they needed it for the weaving. They put it all into their own pockets again, and went on weaving at their looms, which were as empty as ever.

Soon the Emperor sent another honest officer of state to see how the weaving was getting on, and find out if the cloth would soon be ready. Like the Minister before him, the officer of state looked and looked, but as there was nothing on the empty looms he couldn't see anything either.

"Isn't it a fine piece of cloth?" said the two swindlers, and they pretended to show it to him, describing the beautiful pattern which wasn't there at all.

"I'm sure I'm not stupid," thought the officer of state. "So I must be unfit for my job! Well, this is a strange thing indeed, and I mustn't let anyone know about it!" So he praised the cloth he couldn't see, saying how much he liked the fine colors and the beautiful pattern. "Yes, it really is quite exquisite!" he told the Emperor.

All the people in town were talking about that wonderful cloth. So now the Emperor wanted to see it for himself while it was still on the loom. He called on the cunning swindlers with a very select company of courtiers, including the two good old gentlemen who had been to see the cloth before. The two rascals were weaving away with all their might, although there wasn't a single thread on the loom.

"Isn't it superb?" said the Minister and the officer of state. "Oh, your Majesty, just see that pattern and those colors!" And they pointed to the empty loom, believing that everyone else really could see the cloth.

"Goodness me!" thought the Emperor. "I can't see anything at all! This is terrible! Am I stupid? Am I unfit to be Emperor? This is the worst thing that could possibly happen to me!"

However, he said out loud, "Oh yes, it's very beautiful! I like it very much indeed!" And he nodded approvingly at the empty loom. He didn't want to admit that he could see nothing at all. All the courtiers with him stared and stared too, but they couldn't see any more than the Minister and the officer of state. However, they copied the Emperor and said, "Really most attractive!" And they advised him to have the wonderful new cloth made into a suit of clothes to wear in the great procession that was soon to take place. The word went from one to another. "Superb! Exquisite! Excellent!" The courtiers all said how much they liked the cloth, and the Emperor gave the two swindlers decorations to wear in their buttonholes and dubbed them Knights of the Loom.

The two rascally swindlers sat up all night before the day of the procession, with sixteen lights burning, and everyone could see how hard they were working to have the Emperor's new clothes ready in time. They pretended to be taking the cloth off the looms, they snipped their scissors in empty air, they sewed busily away using needles without any thread. Finally they said, "Look, the clothes are ready!"

The Emperor himself arrived, with his most distinguished courtiers, and the two swindlers raised their arms in the air as if they were holding something. "Look, here are the trousers!" they said. "And here's the coat! And here's the cloak! Why," they went on, "it's as light as a cobweb! You might think you were wearing nothing at all, but that's the whole beauty of these clothes!"

"Yes, to be sure!" said all the courtiers, although they still couldn't see anything, because there was nothing to be seen.

"Will Your Imperial Majesty be so gracious as to take your clothes off?" asked the swindlers. "Then we'll dress you in your new ones over there by the big mirror!"

So the Emperor took off all his clothes, and the two swindlers pretended to be dressing him in the new ones they were supposed to have made, fitting them around his waist and acting as if they were putting on the train, while the Emperor turned and preened in front of the mirror. "Oh, how fine those clothes are!" said everyone. "What a perfect fit! What a pattern! What colors! That's a splendid suit of clothes indeed!"

"The canopy that is to be carried over Your Majesty in the procession is waiting outside," said the Master of Ceremonies.

"I'm ready!" said the Emperor. "Don't my clothes suit me well?" And he twisted and turned in front of the mirror once more, pretending to be admiring his fine clothes.

The chamberlains who were to carry the train fumbled on the floor as if they were picking it up, and then pretended to be carrying it. They were afraid to let anyone notice that they couldn't see a thing.

So the Emperor walked in procession under the fine canopy, and all the people in the streets and standing at the windows cried, "Oh, how wonderful the Emperor's new clothes look! What a fine cloak he's wearing over his coat! How well they suit him!" For no one wanted people to think he couldn't see anything. That would have meant he was either stupid or unfit for his job. None of the Emperor's other clothes had ever been so greatly admired.

"But the Emperor has no clothes on!" said a child.

"Listen to the little innocent!" said the child's father.

But the people began passing what the child had said on to each other.

"The Emperor has no clothes! The child over there says the Emperor has no clothes on!"

Finally all the people were shouting, "The Emperor has no clothes on!" And the Emperor cringed, for he thought in his heart they were right, but he said to himself, "I must hold out until the end of the procession." So he bore himself even more proudly than before, and the chamberlains went on carrying the train that wasn't there at all.

The
Princess
& the Pea

*O*nce upon a time there was a prince who wanted to marry a princess, but she had to be a real princess. So he went all around the world looking for one, but there was something the matter everywhere. He met plenty of princesses, but he couldn't be sure whether they were real princesses. There was always something not quite right about them. So he came home again, feeling very sad, because he did so want to marry a real princess.

One evening there was a terrible storm, with thunder and lightning, and the rain poured down. It was really dreadful!

Someone came knocking at the great gate, and the old king went to open it.

There was a princess standing outside, but oh dear, she was in such a state, what with the rain and the terrible storm! Water was dripping from her hair and her clothes, running in at the toes of her shoes and out at the heels again. But she said she was a real princess.

"Well," thought the old queen, "we'll soon see about that!" However, she said nothing, but went into the bedroom, took all the bedclothes off and put a pea on the bedstead.

Then she took twenty mattresses and put them on top of the pea, and after that she put twenty eiderdown quilts on top of the mattresses. That was where the princess was to spend the night.

In the morning, she was asked how she had slept.

"Oh, very badly!" said the princess. "I could hardly sleep a wink all night! Goodness knows what was in my bed! I was lying on something so hard that I'm black and blue all over. It's really terrible!"

So then they could tell she was a real princess, because she had felt the pea through all twenty mattresses and twenty eiderdown quilts. Only a real princess could be as sensitive as that.

Then the prince married her, for now he knew he had found a real princess, and the pea was put in a museum, where it can be seen to this day if nobody has taken it.

There, that was a real story!

The Tinderbox

A soldier came marching down the high road. One, two! One, two! He had his knapsack on his back and a sword at his side, for he had been away fighting in the wars, and now he was going home.

As he went along, he met an old witch on the road. She was very ugly, with a lower lip that hung down to her chest.

"Good evening, soldier!" said she. "What a fine sword you have, and what a big knapsack! I see you are a real soldier indeed. Well now, you can have as much money as you want!"

"Thank you kindly, old witch," said the soldier.

"Do you see that big tree?" asked the witch, pointing to a tree growing near the road. "It's hollow inside! Climb up it and you will see the hole. You can get into that hole and right down inside the tree. I'll tie a rope around your waist, and then I can haul you up when you call me!"

"But what am I to do inside the tree?" asked the soldier.

"Fetch the money!" said the witch. "When you reach the bottom of the tree you will find yourself in a great passage. It is very light, for there are over a hundred lamps burning there. You'll see three doors. You can open them, for the keys are in the locks. Go into the first room, and in the middle of the floor you will see a large chest with a dog sitting on it. He has eyes as big as teacups, but don't let that alarm you. I'll give you my blue check apron. Just spread it on the floor, and then you can march up to the dog, put him on the apron, open the chest and take as much money out of it as you like. The coins in that chest are all copper, but if you would rather have silver, then go into the next room, where you will find a dog with eyes as big as millwheels. However, don't let that alarm you. Just put him on the apron and take the money! And if you would rather have gold, go into the third room and you can take as much of it as you can carry. The dog sitting on the chest of money in the third room has eyes as big as the Round Tower of Copenhagen. He's a remarkable dog and no mistake! But don't let that alarm you. Just put him on the apron; he won't touch you, and you can take as much gold as you like out of the chest!"

"That sounds a pretty good notion!" said the soldier. "But what am I to give you in return, old witch? I'm sure you must want something for yourself!"

"No", said the witch, "not a single coin. I just want you to bring me the old tinderbox my grandmother forgot when she was last down there."

"Well, tie the rope around my waist, then!" said the soldier.

"Here it is," said the witch, "and here's my blue check apron."

So the soldier climbed the tree and let himself down into the hollow trunk. There he was in the great passage with over a hundred lamps burning, exactly as the witch had said.

He opened the first door—and there sat the dog with eyes as big as teacups, glaring at him.

"Nice doggie!" said the soldier, putting him on the witch's apron. He filled his pockets with all the copper coins he could carry, closed the chest again, put the dog back on top of it and went into the next room.

My word! There sat the dog with eyes as big as millwheels.

"Don't you stare at me like that!" said the soldier. "You might do your eyes an injury!" And he put the dog on the witch's apron. When he saw all the silver coins in the chest he threw away the copper he had taken and filled his pockets and his knapsack with pure silver. Then he went on into the third room. That was an alarming sight and no mistake! The dog in there really did have eyes as big as the Round Tower, and they went round and round in his head like wheels.

"Good evening to you," said the soldier, touching his cap respectfully to the dog, for he had never seen such an animal before. He stood and gaped at him for a while, but then he thought, "Well, that's enough of that!" And he picked the dog up, put him on the floor and opened the chest.

Mercy, what a lot of gold it held! Enough to buy the whole of Copenhagen, and the sweetmeat seller's sugar pigs, enough to buy all the tin soldiers and toy whips and rocking horses in the world. This was wealth indeed!

So the soldier emptied his pockets and knapsack of all the silver coins and filled them with gold instead—his pockets, his knapsack, even his cap and boots, so that he could hardly walk. He had plenty of money now! He put the dog back on the chest, closed the door and called up through the hollow tree, "You can haul me up, old witch!"

"Have you found the tinderbox?" asked the witch.

"My word!" said the soldier. "I forgot all about it!" So he went back and found it. Then the witch hauled him up, and there he was, standing in the high road again, with his pockets, his boots, his knapsack, and his cap full of money.

"What do you want that tinderbox for?" asked the soldier.

"Mind your own business," said the witch. "You have your money, so hand over the tinderbox!"

"None of that, now!" said the soldier. "You tell me what you want the tinderbox for, or I'll draw my sword and cut off your head."

"Won't!" said the witch.

So the soldier cut off her head, and there she lay. He tied up all his money in her apron, slung the bundle over his back, put the tinderbox in his pocket, and marched on to the nearest town.

It was a very fine town, and he went into the grandest inn in the place, hired the best room and ordered his favorite food, for he had so much money that he was a rich man now.

The servant who cleaned the shoes thought it strange that a rich man should wear such shabby old boots, but the soldier hadn't had time to get any new ones yet. Next day, however, he bought boots and clothes fit for a fine gentleman, and the townsfolk told him all about their town and their King, and what a lovely girl his daughter the Princess was.

"How can I see her?" asked the soldier.

"Oh, no one can see her!" said the townsfolk. "She lives in a great copper castle surrounded by walls and towers. The King won't let anyone see her but himself, because it has been foretold that she will marry a common soldier, and the King doesn't care for that idea at all."

The soldier thought, "I'd like to see her, all the same." But there was no chance he could do that.

Well, the soldier lived a merry life. He went to the theatre, he drove out in the King's park, and he also gave a great deal of money to the poor, for he remembered what it was like to be penniless. Now that he was rich and wore fine clothes he made a great many friends. They all said he was a good fellow and a real gentleman. That was the kind of thing the soldier liked to hear!

However, he was spending money every day, but no more money was coming in, so he was soon down to his last two coins. He had to move out of the grand room where he had been living and take a little one up in the attics. He brushed and mended his own boots now, and none of his friends came to see him any more. There were so many stairs to climb.

One dark evening, when he could not even afford to buy a candle, he remembered that there was a little candle end in the tinderbox he had fetched up for the witch from the hollow tree. He found the tinderbox and the candle end, but as soon as he struck a spark from the flint the door flew open and in came the dog he had seen in the passage below the tree, the dog with eyes as big as teacups. He stopped in front of the soldier.

"What are your orders, master?" said the dog.

"Upon my word!" said the soldier. "This is a remarkable tinderbox if it means I can order anything I want! Fetch me some money!" he said, and the dog was gone in a twinkling. Next moment he was back again, with a great big bag of coins in his mouth.

Now the soldier realized what a wonderful tinderbox he had! If he struck the flint once, the dog from the chest of copper coins appeared; if he struck it twice, the dog from the chest of silver came; and if he struck it three times, the dog from the chest of gold coins arrived. So the soldier went back to live in his grand room again, and wore fine clothes, and his friends all remembered him and made a great fuss of him.

Well, one day he was thinking, "What a pity it is that no one can see the Princess! Everyone says she's so beautiful, but what's the good of that if she's always kept shut up in a copper castle surrounded by towers? Can't I find some way to see her? Where's my tinderbox?" He struck the flint, and in came the dog with eyes as big as teacups.

"I know it's the middle of the night," said the soldier, "but I would so like to see the Princess, just for a moment!"

The dog went straight out of the door, and before the soldier knew it he was back with the Princess riding on him, still fast asleep. She was so pretty that anyone could see she was a real Princess, and the soldier, who was a real soldier, could not help kissing her.

The dog took the Princess home again. But in the morning, when the King and Queen were drinking tea, she told them that she had dreamed a very strange dream that night, about a dog and a soldier. In her dream she rode on the dog's back and the soldier kissed her.

"Dear me, what a story!" said the Queen.

And one of the old ladies in waiting was told to keep watch by the Princess's bedside the next night, to see if it was really a dream or not.

The soldier longed to see the beautiful Princess again, and so the dog came for her in the night. He ran as fast as he could, but the old lady in waiting put on her boots and followed. She saw the dog go into a large house. "I'll be able to tell the place," she thought, and she took a piece of chalk and drew a cross on the door. Then she went home and lay down, and the dog soon brought the Princess back. But noticing the cross drawn on the door of the soldier's inn, the dog took a piece of chalk too and drew a cross on every door in town. That was very clever, because now that all the doors had crosses on them the lady in waiting couldn't find the right one.

Early in the morning the King, the Queen, the old lady in waiting and all the courtiers went to see where the Princess had been.

"That's it!" said the King, seeing the first door with a cross on it.

"No, my dear, it's this one!" said the Queen, looking at the next door, which also had a cross on it.

"It's this one! No, it's this one!" said everyone. But wherever they looked there were crosses on the doors, so they couldn't tell which one they really wanted.

However, the Queen was a very clever woman who could do more than sit in a state carriage. She took her golden scissors, cut up a piece of silk, and made a pretty little bag of it. She filled the bag with finely ground buckwheat, tied it around the Princess's waist, and then she snipped a little hole in the bag so that the buckwheat could trickle out all along the way, anywhere the Princess went.

The dog came again that night, took the Princess on his back and carried her off to the soldier. He was so much in love with her that he wished he were a Prince, and could have her for his wife.

But the dog never noticed the buckwheat trickling out all the way from the castle to the place where he jumped up on the wall with the Princess and in through the soldier's window. Next morning the King and Queen could tell where their daughter had been, and the soldier was arrested and put in prison.

So there he sat. It was dark and dreary, and they told him he was to be hanged next day. That was not at all amusing, and he had left the tinderbox in his room at the inn.

In the morning, through the iron bars of the little window of his cell, he could see people hurrying out of the town to the place of execution to see him hanged. He heard drums, and saw guards marching by. All the people were going out to see the show. Among the crowd there was a cobbler's apprentice in his leather apron and slippers, running so fast that one of the slippers flew off and fell to the ground near the wall of the prison, where the soldier was peering out through the iron bars.

"Hey, you, cobbler's boy! Don't be in such a hurry," called the soldier. "Nothing's going to happen until I get there! Listen, if you go to the inn where I was staying and fetch me my tinderbox, I'll give you four coins, but you must hurry!"

Well, the cobbler's apprentice wanted to earn four coins, so he ran off to fetch the tinderbox, gave it to the soldier, and then—yes, now we'll see what happened!

A gallows had been set up outside town. It was surrounded by guards and hundreds of thousands of people. The King and the Queen were sitting on a grand throne, with the judge and the whole council opposite.

The soldier had already climbed the ladder, but when they were going to put the noose around his neck he said it was usual for a condemned man to be granted one last wish before he died. He would very much like to smoke a pipe of tobacco, he said, the last pipe he would ever smoke in this world.

The King could hardly refuse him, so the soldier brought out his tinderbox and struck the flint—once, twice, three times. And there were all the dogs: the dog with eyes as big as teacups, the dog with eyes as big as millwheels, and the dog with eyes as big as the Round Tower of Copenhagen.

"Come along, help me. I don't want to be hanged!" said the soldier, and the dogs raced toward the judge and the council, seizing one man by the leg and another by the nose, and tossed them all so high into the air that when they came down they broke into pieces.

"Leave me alone!" said the King, but the biggest dog seized him and the Queen and tossed them up in the air too, after all the others. The guards were terrified, and all the people shouted, "Little soldier, we want you to be our King and marry the beautiful Princess!"

So the soldier drove in the King's carriage, and all three dogs pranced in front of it shouting, "Hooray!" and boys whistled on their fingers, and the guards presented arms. The Princess came out of her copper castle and became Queen, and she liked that very much indeed! The wedding festivities went on for a week, and the dogs sat at the table with the other guests, staring around them with their great big eyes.

The Rose Tree Regiment

There was a rose tree standing in the window. Not long ago it had been young and healthy, but now it looked sickly, and had something wrong with it.

There were soldiers billeted on it, eating it all up—men of honor they were, wearing green uniforms.

I talked to one of the soldiers billeted on the rose tree. He was only three days old, but he was already a great-grandfather. Do you know what he said? He told me about himself and all the others living in those quarters, and every word he said was true.

"We are the most remarkable regiment of creatures on earth. In the summer we bear live young, for the weather is good then; we get engaged and then married at once. In the cold weather we lay eggs, and the little ones are nice and cozy. That wisest of creatures, the ant, whom we respect deeply, studies us and knows our worth. The ants do not eat us at once, but take our eggs and put them in the family anthill on the ground floor, stacked layer upon layer so they can hatch out. Then they put us in a stable, squeeze our hind legs and milk us until we die. It's a real pleasure, I assure you! They give us the nicest of names; they call us 'sweet little milk cow.' All creatures as intelligent as ants call us by that name, except for humans, and that hurts our feelings and makes us feel bad. Can't you write about it, by the way, and show humans their mistake? They look at us in such a stupid way, glaring at us just because we eat rose leaves, while they themselves eat all living creatures and everything green that grows. They give us the most contemptuous name, the most disgusting name; I won't say it! Yuk! It turns my stomach! I just can't say it, or at least not in uniform, and I always wear uniform.

"I was born among rose leaves, I and the whole regiment live on the rose tree, but you could say it lives on in us, for we belong to the higher orders of creatures. Humans don't like us; they come and kill us with soapsuds. What a nasty drink! I think I can smell it now. It's horrible to be washed when you weren't born to be washed!

"Humans! Listen, you there, staring at me with that nasty soapy look in your eyes; remember our place in Nature and the clever way we can lay eggs and bear live young! We were blessed and told to go forth and multiply. We live on roses, we die in roses; our whole life is poetry. Don't call us by that disgusting, nasty name—I won't say it, I absolutely will not utter the word! Call us the ant's cows, the rose tree regiment, the little green ones!"

As one of the human race, I stood and looked at the rose tree and the little green ones, the rose tree regiment. I won't mention their name either, or hurt the feelings of any of the citizens of the rose tree, a great family which can lay eggs and bear live young. As for the soapsuds I was going to throw over them—for I had indeed fetched soapsuds with evil intent—I will whip them into foam, blow soap bubbles, gaze at their beauty, and there may be a fairy tale in it.

I blew a big, brightly colored bubble, with a silver bead at the bottom of it. My bubble rose, hovered, floated to the door and burst. The door flew open, and there stood Old Mother Fairy Tale herself.

Well, she can tell the story better than I can, the story about—no, I won't say their name—the story about the rose tree regiment!

"Leaf lice!" said Old Mother Fairy Tale. "You should call things by their true names, and even if you don't do so in the usual way, that's what you ought to do in a fairy tale."

The Naughty Boy

*O*nce upon a time there was an old poet, and a really good old man he was too. One evening, when he was sitting at home, there was a terrible storm outside and the rain poured down in torrents. However, the old poet was warm and comfortable sitting by the fire that burned in his stove, with apples roasting in it.

"Any poor folk out in this storm can't have a dry stitch left on them!" said he, for as I told you, he was a good old man.

"Let me in!" cried a little boy outside. "I'm freezing, and it's so wet!" He was weeping and knocking at the door, while the rain went on pouring down and the wind rattled all the windows.

"Why, the poor little creature!" said the old poet, and he went and opened the door. There stood a little boy, stark naked, with water dripping from his long yellow hair. He was shivering with cold, and if he hadn't been let indoors he would surely have died in that terrible storm.

"You poor child!" said the old poet, taking his hand. "Come along in and I'll get you warm! You shall have wine to drink and roasted apples to eat. What a pretty boy you are!"

And indeed, so he was. His eyes were bright as stars, and though water was streaming from his yellow hair it curled in a very charming way. He looked like a little cherub, but he was white with cold and trembling all over. He was carrying a nice little bow and arrows. However, the rain had spoiled them, making all the colors of the pretty arrows run.

The old poet sat down by the stove, took the little boy on his lap, dried his hair, warmed his hands between his own, and gave him sweet wine to drink. The little boy soon recovered. His cheeks grew rosy, and he jumped down to the floor and danced around the old poet.

"You're a merry child!" said the old man. "What's your name?"

"My name is Cupid!" said the boy. "Don't you know me? Here's my bow and arrows! You should just see me shoot with them! Look, the storm's cleared up outside and the moon is shining!"

"But your bow is spoiled!" said the old poet.

"What a shame!" said the little boy, picking it up and looking at it. "Oh no, it's dry again now, and it's not damaged! The string is taut! Let me try it!" And so saying he bent the bow, put an arrow to the string, took aim and shot the good old poet right in the heart. "There, now you see my bow isn't spoiled!" he said, and he laughed out loudly and ran away.

What a naughty little boy he was, to shoot the old poet who had taken him into his warm room and was so kind to him, giving him good wine to drink and delicious apples to eat!

The good old poet lay on the floor, weeping, for he had been wounded deeply in the heart. "Oh, what a naughty boy Cupid is!" he said. "I'll tell all good children to be on their guard and never play with him, for he will do them great harm!"

And all the good children to whom he told his tale, both girls and boys, were on their guard against that naughty boy Cupid, but he tricked them all the same, for he's a cunning creature! When students come out of lectures he will walk along beside them in a black gown, with a book under his arm. They don't recognize him, so they link arms with him, taking him for another student, and then he shoots his arrows into their breasts. He is on the watch for girls when they have been to see the priest and when they are in church. He is always chasing people! He sits up in the great chandelier in the theater, shining so brightly that folks think he is one of the lights in it, but they soon discover their mistake. He walks in the King's park and down all the garden paths. Once upon a time he even shot your mother and father in the heart. Just ask them, and see what they say! Yes, Cupid is a naughty boy, and you should have nothing to do with him. He pursues everyone. Why, he once shot an arrow at your old grandmother, but that's a long time ago now. All the same, she has never forgotten it. Shame on you, Cupid! Well, now you will recognize him when you meet him—and you must agree, he is a very naughty boy!

The Jumpers

*O*nce upon a time the flea, the grasshopper, and the jumping jack wanted to find out which of them could jump the highest, and they invited the world and his wife to see the show. When the three of them were in the room together you could tell that they were all really good at jumping.

"I'll give my daughter to whoever jumps highest!" said the King. "It would be a shame for them to jump for nothing!"

The flea came forward first. He had elegant manners and nodded to all present, for he had noble blood in him and was accustomed to mixing in human society, and that meant a good deal.

Next came the grasshopper, who was considerably stouter, but looked very fine in the green uniform he wore. Moreover, he said he came of a very old family in the land of Egypt, and was highly thought of over here as well. He came from the fields, and now he lived in a house of cards three stories high. The cards used to build it showed the Kings and Knaves, with the colored pictures on the inside, and the doors and windows were cut out of cards showing the Queen of Hearts. "I sing so well," said he, "that sixteen native crickets who have chirped from youth, but don't live in a house of cards, have been so annoyed by hearing me that they became even thinner than they were before!"

Both the flea and the grasshopper spoke highly of their own talents, and said they thought they were fit to marry a Princess.

As for the jumping jack, he said nothing, but folks believed that meant he was thinking all the harder, and when the court dog sniffed him he said he was sure the jumping jack came from a good family. The old councillor who had been given three decorations for keeping silent said that he saw the jumping jack had the gift of prophecy: you could tell from his back whether it was going to be a mild winter or a harsh one, which is more than you can tell from the back of the man who writes the almanac.

"Well, I won't say anything!" said the old King. "But I can think what I like!"

Now it was time for the jumping to begin. The flea jumped so high that no one could see him, so they said he hadn't jumped at all, and he was cheating.

The grasshopper jumped only half as high as the flea, but he jumped right in the King's face, and the King said that was nasty.

The jumping jack stood there silent for some time, thinking the matter over, until people thought he couldn't jump at all.

"I hope he doesn't feel sick!" said the court dog, sniffing him again. Whoosh! the jumping jack gave a little leap and landed in the lap of the Princess, who was sitting on a low golden stool.

Then the King said, "The highest jump was the jump up to my daughter, for you can't go any higher. But it took a quick wit to find that out, and the jumping jack is clever and has brains."

So he had won the Princess.

"But I jumped highest!" said the flea. "Still, it comes to the same thing! Let her have the jumping jack for all I care! I jumped the highest, but it seems looks are all that count in this world!"

So the flea went abroad on active service, and they say that he was killed.

The grasshopper went and sat down in the ditch and thought about the way of the world, and he agreed: "Looks are all that count! Looks are all that count!" And so he sang his own sad song, and I wrote this story about it. You needn't believe every word, even though you've seen it in print.

The Little
Match Girl

*I*t was bitterly cold; snow was falling, and it was beginning to get dark. This was the last evening of the year, New Year's Eve. A poor little girl was walking through the streets in the cold and the dark. Her head and feet were bare. She had been wearing slippers when she left home, but that did her no good now! They were far too big for her—they were really her mother's slippers, and they were so big that they came off as the little girl hurried over the road to get out of the way of two carriages driving along at high speed. When the carriages had passed she couldn't find one of the slippers at all, and a boy ran off with the other, saying he would use it for a cradle when he had a child himself.

So now the little girl was walking along with nothing on her feet, which were red and blue with cold. She had some matches in her apron, and she was holding another bundle of matches, but no one had bought any from her all day long. No one had given her a penny. Hungry and chilled to the bone, the poor little thing went on her way, a picture of misery. The snowflakes fell on her long yellow hair. It curled nicely on her neck, but she never gave her own pretty looks a thought. Lights were shining in all the windows, and there was a delicious smell of roast goose in the streets, for this was New Year's Eve. She did think about that.

She sat down in a corner between two houses, one of them standing out farther into the street than the other, and curled her little legs up under her, but now she felt even colder than before. She dared not go home because she had sold no matches. She hadn't earned a penny, and she was afraid her father would beat her. It was cold at home too; the place was only an attic, and although the biggest chinks in the roof were stuffed with straw and rags, the wind still came in. Her little hands were numb with cold. Perhaps the flame of a match would do them good! Dare she take one out of the bundle, strike it on the wall and warm her fingers? She did; she drew one out, struck it—and oh, how it sparkled and burned! It gave a warm, clear light like a little candle. She cupped her hand around it. What a strange light it was! The little girl felt as if she were sitting by a big iron stove decorated with shiny brass balls and bars, and a lovely warm fire burning in it. She stretched out her feet to get them warm them too—but then the flame went out. The iron stove disappeared, and there she sat with the tiny end of the burnt match in her hand.

She struck another match. It burned and shone, and where its light fell the wall seemed to become transparent as a veil, so that she could see into the room inside. There was a table laid with a spotless white cloth, fine china, and a roast goose stuffed with prunes and apples, which smelled delicious. Better still, the goose jumped off its dish, although it had a knife and fork stuck in it, and waddled across the floor toward the little girl. But then the match went out, and there was nothing to be seen but the hard, cold wall.

She struck a third match, and now she was sitting under a beautiful Christmas tree, much bigger and more handsomely decorated than the one she had seen through the rich merchant's glass doors on Christmas Eve. A thousand candles were burning on the green branches, and brightly colored figures such as you see in shop windows looked down on her. The little girl reached both hands out in the air—but then the match went out. The flames of all the Christmas candles burned higher and higher, and she saw that they were bright stars. One of them fell leaving a fiery trail in the sky behind it.

"Someone is dying," said the little girl, for her old grandmother used to say that when a star falls a soul is going to God. Her grandmother, who was dead now, was the only person who had ever been kind to her.

She struck another match on the wall. It flared up, and in its light she saw her old grandmother herself, bright, shining and kind. What a welcome sight that was!

"Oh, Grandmother!" called the little girl. "Take me with you! I know you'll go when the match goes out, like the warm stove, the delicious roast goose and the beautiful big Christmas tree!" And she hastily struck all the rest of the matches in her bundle to keep her grandmother there. The matches burned with such a light, it was brighter than the day. Her grandmother had never looked so tall and beautiful before. She picked the little girl up in her arms and they flew away in joy and glory, up and up, going to the place where there is no cold or hunger or pain any more, going to be with God.

The little girl was found in the corner between the two houses in the cold light of dawn. Her cheeks were red and there was a smile on her lips, but she was dead, frozen to death on the last evening of the Old Year. The sun of New Year's Day rose over the little body as she sat there with the bundle of burnt matches. "Trying to keep warm," they said. No one knew what beautiful visions she had seen, or how she and her old grandmother had gone away into the glory and joy of the New Year.

Also illustrated by *Lisbeth Zwerger* from *Picture Book Studio:*

Aesop's Fables

The Nightingale
The Swineherd
Thumbeline
by Hans Christian Andersen

The Legend of Rosepetal
by Clemens Brentano

A Christmas Carol
by Charles Dickens

Hansel and Gretel
Little Red Cap
The Seven Ravens
by The Brothers Grimm

The Gift of the Magi
by O. Henry

The Nutcracker
The Strange Child
by E.T. A Hoffmann

The Merry Pranks of Till Eulenspiegel
by Heinz Janisch

The Deliverers of Their Country
by Edith Nesbit

The Canterville Ghost
The Selfish Giant
by Oscar Wilde